For Dimitri —A.L.

For Oli —G.D.

Carolrhoda Books®
An imprint of Lerner Publishing Group, Inc.
241 First Avenue North
Minneapolis, MN 55401 USA

For reading levels and more information, look up this title at www.lernerbooks.com.

Cover font: anmark/Shutterstock.

Designed by Danielle Carnito.
Main body text set in Sassoon Primary Std.
Typeface provided by Monotype Typography.
The illustrations in this book were created digitally with an iPad and Wacom tablet.

Library of Congress Cataloging-in-Publication Data

Names: Limón, Ada, author. | D'Alessandro, Gaby, illustrator.
Title: And, too, the fox / Ada Limón ; illustrated by Gaby D'Alessandro.
Description: Minneapolis : Carolrhoda Books, 2025. | Audience: Ages 6–10. | Audience: Grades 2–3. | Summary: Brief text and lush illustrations are paired in this joyous poem about a fox.
Identifiers: LCCN 2023050845 (print) | LCCN 2023050846 (ebook) | ISBN 9798765639252 (library binding) | ISBN 9798765639276 (epub)
Subjects: LCSH: Foxes—Juvenile poetry. | Children's poetry, American. | CYAC: Foxes—Poetry. | American poetry. | LCGFT: Animal poetry. | Picture books.
Classification: LCC PS3612.I496 A53 2025 (print) | LCC PS3612.I496 (ebook) | DDC 811/.6—dc23/eng/20240130

LC record available at https://lccn.loc.gov/2023050845
LC ebook record available at https://lccn.loc.gov/2023050846

Manufactured in Guang Dong, China by Dream Colour Printing
1-1010245-52317-4/15/2024

And, Too, the Fox

U.S. Poet Laureate **Ada Limón** with art by **Gaby D'Alessandro**

CAROLRHODA BOOKS
MINNEAPOLIS

Comes with its streak of red

flashing across the lawn,

squirrel bound

and bouncing

almost as if it were effortless to hunt,

food being
an afterthought
or
just a little boring.

He doesn't say a word.

Just uses those four black feet

to silently go about

his work,

which doesn't seem

like work at all but play.

Fox lives on the edges,

pieces together

a living out of leftovers

and lazy
rodents too slow for the telephone pole.

He takes only what he needs

and lives a life that some might
call small,

has a few friends,

likes the grass when it's soft and green,

never cares how long you watch,

never cares what you need
when you're watching,

never cares

what you do once he is gone.